Zoey
AND
SASSAFRAS

MERHORSES AND BUBBLES

THE INNOVATION PRESS

READ THE REST OF THE SERIES

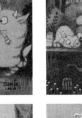

for activities and more visit

ZOEYANDSASSAFRAS.COM

TABLE OF CONTENTS

FOR ELLIE AND LUCY — ML
FOR GOOSE AND BUBS — AC

Publisher's Cataloging-in-Publication
Citro, Asia, author.
Merhorses and bubbles / Asia Citro ; illustrator, Marion Lindsay.
pages cm -- (Zoey and Sassafras ; 3)
Summary: A girl, Zoey, and her cat, Sassafras, use science experiments to help a local stream and magical merhorses.
Audience: Grades K-5.
LCCN 2016904047
ISBN 978-1-943147-19-9; ISBN 978-1-943147-18-2; ISBN 978-1-943147-20-5;
ISBN 978-1-943147-21-2; ISBN 978-1-943147-22-9
1. Cats--Juvenile fiction. 2. Animals, Mythical--Juvenile fiction. 3. Horses--Juvenile fiction.
4. Aquatic ecology--Juvenile fiction. [1. Cats--Fiction. 2. Imaginary creatures--Fiction.
3. Horses--Fiction. 4. Ecology--Fiction. 5. Science--Experiments--Fiction. 6. Experiments--
Fiction.] I. Lindsay, Marion, illustrator. II. Title. III. Series: Citro, Asia. Zoey and Sassafras
PZ7.1.C577Mo 2016
[E]
QBI16-600079

Text copyright 2017 by Asia Citro
Illustrations copyright 2017 by Marion Lindsay
Journal entries handwritten by S. Citro

Published by The Innovation Press
1001 4th Avenue, Suite 3200, Seattle, WA 98154
www.theinnovationpress.com

Printed and bound by Worzalla
Production Date: June 2021 | Plant Location: Stevens Point, Wisconsin

Cover design by Nicole LaRue | Book layout by Kerry Ellis

PROLOGUE

These days my cat Sassafras and I are always desperately hoping we'll hear our barn doorbell.

I know most people are excited to hear their doorbell ring. It might mean a present or package delivery, or a friend showing up to play. But our doorbell is even more exciting than that. Because it's a *magic* doorbell. When it rings, it means there's a magical animal waiting outside our barn. A magical animal who needs our help.

My mom's been helping them basically her whole life. And now *I* get to help too . . .

CHAPTER 1
LOOKING UNDERWATER

A shadow caught my eye and I ran to the window. Was that –? No, it was just a crow. I sighed.

Our baby dragon friend, Marshmallow, had returned to his life in the forest weeks ago. But I was hoping he'd come visit again soon. Really soon. The sooner the better.

I sighed and rolled a giant tube back and forth on our dining room table with one hand while I searched the sky for Marshmallow. Just in case.

"Ow! Hey, that's my hand!" I yelped.

Sassafras must have been aiming for the rolling tube, which he probably thought was now alive. But his needle-sharp claws landed on my poor hand instead.

"You're not even supposed to be on the table, stinker," I said as I lowered him to my lap.

"Meow!" he complained. He slipped his

front paws onto the table one at a time and looked up to see if I'd noticed.

I had, but I decided to let him stay and watch. "Just a little longer before we go to the stream, Sass. With my underwater viewer, I'll be able to see all the bugs at the bottom of the stream really well. I'll be the best stream bug hunter ever."

Argh! The piece of plastic wrap I'd grabbed from the kitchen wasn't big enough to fit over the end of the tube. I picked up Sassafras and set him on my chair. I patted his head. "I'll be right back and *then* we can go."

I pulled the plastic wrap out of the kitchen drawer and heard a loud yowl from the dining room.

"Meeooooooowww!"

I shook my head. That silly cat. I checked the dining room, but I didn't see Sassafras anywhere.

Thunk.

I looked down at the floor. Something

moved. The plastic tube for my underwater viewer was now *under* the table. How did that get there? I bent down to pick it up, and it turned toward me. My cat's face peered at me from inside the tube.

"Oh, Sassafras! You're not supposed to shove your whole head inside the viewer!

You just *look* through it." I gently wiggled the plastic cylinder off my cat's fluffy head.

His head popped out and he rubbed against me and purred.

"You're welcome, goofball," I said, ruffling his fur. "Maybe we should leave the underwater viewer to me from now on, huh?"

"Meow!" Sassafras agreed.

We sat back down at the dining room table and I got to work. My mom had cut the bottom off a plastic jar to make it a tube with an opening big enough for me to look through. (And also big enough for my cat to get his head caught in.)

I carefully smoothed the plastic wrap over one end of the tube and stretched three rubber bands around the outside. Ta-da! My viewer was done. Now all I needed was some stream water.

I gathered up my things and heard the bushes rustle outside. I ran to the window, hoping that it might be my monster friend Gorp, but this time it was only a squirrel. I sighed. Should I stay home? In case the magic doorbell rang?

Sassafras bumped his head into my leg and meowed impatiently.

He was right. Waiting wasn't going to make a magical creature appear. Besides, I might be even more likely to run into Gorp in the forest. And I could see the sky just as well (and maybe even better) down at the stream. I made up my mind.

"Mom! Dad!" I hollered. "Sassafras and I are going to the stream now."

"OK!" Mom called back. "But remember, no whining when I call you back for lunch!"

"Who me?" I giggled as I headed out the door.

CHAPTER 2
STREAM BUGS

Sassafras ran by my heels and meowed up at me. I could tell that he was especially excited to head to the stream today after all my talk of bug-hunting.

"*If* you promise not to eat them, I'll show you some of my favorite stream bugs," I told him.

Sassafras tilted his head to the side, like he was considering my offer. I really hoped he could resist gobbling up the poor stream bugs. Whenever he spies a bug, his tail gets all twitchy. He's always trying to eat them, and I'm always trying to save them!

"You'll be able to see their neat little gills flutter like hummingbird wings. It's pretty cool, Sassafras. The mayfly babies have *seven* rows of gills down the sides of their bodies. They beat up and down to move the water around and grab teeny tiny bubbles of air out of the water." I took a deep breath. "I do like having lungs, but sometimes I wish I had gills so I could live underwater. Don't you?"

Sassafras' eyes got big. He was probably thinking of all the bugs he'd get to eat if he could breathe underwater.

When we got to the stream, I set all of my supplies on the sandy shore. Today was nice and warm. A perfect day to hunt for stream bugs. The water sparkled as the sun reflected off the ripples in the stream. Wait a minute. Was part of the stream sparkling in rainbow colors? I took a few steps closer and squinted in the sunlight. But I couldn't see the rainbow anymore.

"Huh. I'm so desperate to find magic today, I guess I'm seeing things!" I said to Sassafras. He peered up at me and blinked.

I looked one more time, but the stream seemed normal again. I shrugged and took off my shoes, rolled up my pants, and grabbed my underwater viewer.

"It's bug time!" I exclaimed as I marched into the stream.

Sassafras must have been distracted by the thought of bugs because he followed me. But when the tip of his front paw touched the stream water, he jumped sideways and shook his paw like crazy! He squeezed his eyes closed tight and jumped around a bunch more with his ears flat against his head. I couldn't help but laugh as he flipped and flopped about. Sassafras seriously hates getting wet. Apparently even more than he *loves* eating bugs.

Sassafras climbed a nearby tree and

scowled down at me.

I grabbed the little tub I'd brought and filled it with some stream water. "I'll put the mayfly babies in here, Sassafras. That way I can bring them on shore to show you. But remember. *No eating!*"

I pressed the plastic-wrapped side of my underwater viewer into the water and peered through the tube. I could see the bottom of the stream really clearly. Ooh, a rock as big as Sassafras' head! There ought to be *at least* five or six stream bugs clinging to the bottom of that one. I

flipped it over and saw . . . *nothing*? Huh.
That was weird. The rock was perfect for
stream bugs! I shrugged and used my
underwater viewer to find another big
rock. No bugs.

"What is going on?" I muttered.

I investigated rock after rock after
rock, but I couldn't find a single mayfly
baby. I did, however, find *a lot* of algae.
It was cold and slimy, and I had to keep

flicking my hands to get it off.

I also found some wormlike things oozing along the bottoms of the rocks. I poked at them a little, but they weren't as interesting to watch as my fluttering, gilled mayfly babies.

"Sassafras? Do you think the mayfly babies somehow turned into adult mayflies all at once?" I called up to him. "Mayflies start as eggs, and then the eggs hatch underwater and the little mayfly babies crawl out. They live in the stream for a long time until they get bigger and shed their skin."

I shivered. The shedding skin thing always kind of freaked me out.

"When they get rid of their skin at the top of the water, they crawl out, and *boom* — they have wings. Maybe they did that all at once or something?"

I looked around and didn't see any flying bugs. But then again, mayfly adults only live for a day or so, which is so unfair.

If I lived all my life underwater and woke up with wings one day, I'd want more than *one* day to fly around.

"OK, fine. Maybe all the mayfly babies have flown away. I'll just find you a caddisfly baby, Sassafras. They are also super cool. You can't really see their gills, but they build homes on their backs out of mud and rocks or

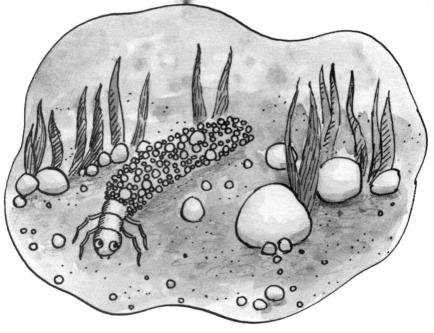

leaves or twigs, and then they can hide inside like a hermit crab hides inside its shell."

I must have made Sassafras curious. He hopped down from the tree and came to the edge of the stream to watch me. I used my underwater viewer to focus on the tops of rocks and the gravelly bottom of the stream this time. But no matter which way I looked, I couldn't find any caddisfly babies crawling around. Was this a really unlucky day?

I flicked more algae off my hand. "Ugh! I give up!" I humphed as I flopped down next to Sassafras on the shore. He nuzzled my arm. We were both pretty bummed. No fun stream bugs today, I guess.

Sassafras' ears pricked toward home. He meowed once and trotted back down the trail. I strained my ears and could barely make out my mom's voice. Oh! It was time for lunch.

As I put my socks and shoes on, I thought I saw that shimmer of rainbow light on the other side of the stream. I took a step closer, but then it disappeared. Mom kept calling in the distance. I took one last minute to look for the rainbow light, but all I saw was the normal sparkling stream water. I shrugged. I must have imagined it. Ugh. There really wasn't *anything* exciting to see at the stream today.

I trudged home with slumped shoulders. So much for a fun afternoon.

CHAPTER 3
STREAM TROUBLE

My mom and dad were getting lunch ready in the kitchen. I sank down in my chair at the table with a frown on my face.

"What's wrong, Zoey? Didn't you have fun at the stream?" Dad asked, taking the seat next to me.

I shook my head no. "I looked and looked, but there were no stream bug babies *anywhere*."

"You mean nymphs?" Mom called over her shoulder.

"Oh, right!" That's the word I kept

forgetting. *Nymphs.* "Yeah, no mayfly or caddisfly nymphs anywhere. Seriously. I'm super good at bug-hunting – I even had my underwater viewer! I guess they all turned into adults at the same time and flew away." I sighed loudly.

My mom stopped what she was doing and sat down with me and Dad. I sat up a little straighter in my chair. "No, they wouldn't all turn to adults at the same time," she said. "That's why we usually find different-sized

nymphs when we go. Some are newly hatched and tiny, and others are about to become adults and huge. Did you see anything else unusual? Like a lot of algae?"

I rubbed my hands on my pants at the thought of it. "Yes, it was super slimy and cold. It kept sticking to my hands."

Mom and Dad looked at each other. Why were they so serious?

Then Mom said, "Sweetie, we need you to wash your hands and feet really well."

"My feet too?" I whined. My stomach growled. "Can't I do it after I eat? Why do I have to do it now?"

"Do you remember your mom telling you why our stream has so many mayfly and caddisfly nymphs?" Dad asked.

I nodded. "Yes, because our stream is really clean. Mayfly and caddisfly babies are delicate. They can only live in waters that aren't polluted with yucky chemicals." My eyes got big as I realized what my dad was trying to say. "Oh no. Is our stream polluted? Are all the baby stream bugs dead?"

Dad shrugged. "We don't know yet. But this doesn't sound good."

"After lunch, you and Sassafras can go back to get a water sample," Mom said. "We can run some tests to check. But right now we need you to wash up."

I went to wash my hands and feet without any more complaining. As I scrubbed my hands, I felt worried. What if our beautiful stream was sick?

CHAPTER 4
WATER TESTS

After a sad and quiet lunch, Sassafras and I went back to the stream. I brought a cup for a water sample and my science journal. When we got there, I took out my journal and wrote:

QUESTION:
Is our stream polluted?

OBSERVATIONS:

No mayfly babies.
No caddisfly babies ☹

I bent over and scooped up some stream water with the cup. This time, I was careful not to get any water on my hands or feet. I tucked my journal under my arm, and Sassafras and I walked straight back home.

We found Mom in her office with Dad. I handed her the water sample I'd carried home from the stream.

"Thanks, sweetie. Do you want to help me?"

I darted over to Mom's side. I was

excited to help. And also a little scared of what the tests might tell us. I was just as worried about the stream bugs as I'd be about any magical animals. Now that I thought about it, I hoped the polluted stream wasn't hurting the magical creatures in the forest too! "There's still a chance that the stream isn't polluted, right, Mom?"

"Yes. We won't know until we run some tests." She put kits with tubes and little tablets on the counter. I peeked at the supplies. I loved when my mom let me use the same tools that real grown-up scientists use in their labs.

I poked a finger at one of the shiny plastic cards with different colored squares. Mom looked down at me. "You're going to use real chemicals to test the water sample. So what do you need for your eyes?"

"My Thinking Goggles!" I dashed to my room, grabbed my lucky goggles, and ran back to help my mom. I usually wore my Thinking Goggles on top of my head (close to my brain) to give me good ideas. But this time I used them in the usual way – on the front of my face to keep my eyes safe.

Mom opened a tiny tube filled with little strips of paper. "Let's test for pH first. Put on the gloves, then fill an empty test tube with some of the stream water. Next, add a strip of paper and watch it. It will change color after about a minute. Once the color stops changing, pull it out and match it to one of the colored squares on this card."

I did all the things she said. It took me a minute to decide which square matched the color of the paper strip. "I'm pretty sure it matches square number ten. What does that mean, Mom?"

Dad shook his head sadly.

"It means that there's definitely something in our stream," Mom said. "A normal stream would be close to seven.

Pollution can cause that number to go really low or really high, depending on what is being added. This is a clue, though. We know that whatever was added to the stream has a high pH number. Let's run one more test to see if we can guess what type of pollution it is."

She pulled out a new test tube. This time I got to put a tablet inside the tube and shake it. The stream water changed from clear to a pretty blue in the tube.

Mom and Dad both frowned when they saw the color.

"It's testing positive for phosphates," Mom said to Dad. Then she turned to me. "These results definitely explain why you didn't see any mayfly or caddisfly nymphs. My best guess is that there's some kind of soap or detergent getting into our stream."

I set the tube down with a frown and

wrote in my science journal:

DATA:

pH = 10, something bad is in our stream.

Tablet = some kind of soap is in our stream.

CONCLUSION:

Our stream is polluted 😦

Just then the doorbell rang. But not the regular doorbell. The *magic* one.

CHAPTER 5

MAGIC DOORBELL

Mom and I looked at each other and froze.

"Is that some kind of reminder alarm on your phone?" Dad asked my mom.

"Um, sort of," Mom replied.

The doorbell meant that a magical creature needed our help. But my dad couldn't see the creatures. To him, it looked like nothing was there. This was going to be a bit tricky.

I looked at my mom and raised my eyebrows.

"Zoey, I think I left something out in the barn?" My mom raised an eyebrow back at me.

"Oh, right, that *thing*," I said. "Sassafras and I can get it for you."

Sassafras and I dashed outside and through the barn to the back door. I opened it and looked around. My shoulders dropped. No one was there.

Then I looked *way* down. I jumped in surprise. There on the grass, standing on two legs like a person, was a shimmering purple frog covered head to toe in neon spots.

Could it be? Was this the talking frog my mom had told me stories about?

Sassafras pushed in front of me. He closed his eyes and gently bumped his head against the frog.

The frog reached out a tiny webbed hand and petted Sassafras on the nose. "Hello, old friend!"

Sassafras immediately began purring. "Pip? Is that really you?" I squeaked. The frog looked up at me. "You can see me . . . *and* you know my name? Who *are* you?"

Ever since I'd seen a picture of Pip in my mom's office, I'd been dying to meet him. I burst out with everything all at once. "Hi, Pip! I'm Zoey. I think you were expecting my mom? But I can see you too. I've been helping my mom with the magical animals. Are you hurt? Is

something wrong?"

"Oh my. Let's see here. First, hi, Zoey. Nice to meet you. I *was* expecting your mom. But you will do." Pip took a deep breath and got a serious look on his face. "The merhorses from our stream are in trouble. We don't know what's wrong."

Pip began talking faster and faster. "Their skin and eyes hurt, and they can't

find any of their food. They usually eat mooflies, but they can't find any."

"*Mayflies?*"

"Right! They said they can't find the marchflies under the water anymore." He paused in thought for a moment and scratched his head. "Although I'm not sure what that means. I don't know of any flies that live underwater."

"Well, *mayflies* start their lives underwater as babies," I said. "They have gills and stuff until they get way bigger. Then they actually fly."

"Huh. Well, anyway, there's something going on, because all the merflies are missing!"

"I noticed that the *mayflies* were missing when I was at the stream earlier," I said. "Mom and I just finished running some tests on the stream water. I've got some bad news. It's polluted."

"Oh no," said Pip, placing two tiny webbed hands on his cheeks. "I need to see your mother right away!"

Then Pip jumped onto my head!

"Ah, that's much better. Humans are so useful. I can always see better from up here. What are you waiting for? Take me to her!"

I walked back to my house as quickly as I could manage with a frog on my head and a nervous cat winding through my legs. When I opened the front door, I wondered what would happen with my dad there. He couldn't see anything magical. How would we talk to Pip? Maybe I should wait until later?

"Zoey?" called Mom from her office. "Did you, um, find the *thing*?"

Uh oh, too late to turn back now. They'd heard me come in. I cleared my throat. "Yeah. I definitely found something."

I turned the corner and my mom's jaw dropped.

"Pip? Is that you?" she said.

"Did you teach Zoey your pretend frog game?" Dad asked. "In that case, I'll take my own pretend frog to make a snack for us and leave you two to play with yours." He held out his hand and looked at it. "Hello, Plop! It's time for an afternoon snack. Would you like to come help me? Yes? Oh, thanks." Dad leaned in closer to his empty hand. "Sure, Plop! We can make some dead fly sandwiches for you and your friend Pip."

On my head, Pip spluttered in disgust. "I

would never eat a dead insect. Disgusting!"
Mom and I bit our lips to keep from laughing.

We had to work hard to hear Dad over Pip's
shouting. "Plop and I will be in the kitchen.
Will you three … I mean *four* … join us soon?"

Mom cleared her throat. "Let us clean
up in here first. Then we'll come join you."

Dad nodded and left, carefully
carrying his handful of air.

My mom turned back to Pip, who
had hopped down to her desk. He was
standing there with his arms crossed.

"Ugh." He sighed. "I thought he'd never
leave. And really, *Plop*? What kind of a
name is that?"

"I'm so glad to see you, Pip." Mom
kissed him gently on the head.

"I'm glad to see you too," Pip said. "But
we need to get to work."

Mom frowned. "I was hoping you came
to visit. Is something wrong in the forest?"

Pip flailed his arms around. "It's the
merhorses. They have red spots all over
their skin and scales. They're having

trouble breathing and their eyes hurt. They can't find enough food. And Zoey says the stream is *polluted*?"

Mom clapped a hand to her mouth. "Of course, the other creatures in the stream must be suffering, including the magical ones. Those poor merhorses!"

Seeing my mom so upset made my stomach hurt a little. What were we going to do?

CHAPTER 6
THE MERHORSES

Mom and I hurried through the snack that Dad and "Plop" had made. Pip sat on my head. He kept fidgeting, which was very distracting.

"I think Zoey and I are going to head back to the stream," said Mom. "I'd like to see if we can find the source of the pollution."

"Absolutely," Dad said. "I'll come with you guys. Three pairs of eyes are better than two, right?"

Mom and I exchanged worried looks. Pip wanted to take us to the merhorses so we could talk to them. How could we do that with my dad there? It would look like we were talking to air again. After our conversation with Pip earlier, it might be too much for Dad.

Mom's eyes lit up. "That would be great! Why don't you and I go upstream, and Zoey can go downstream. We'll meet again at the middle?"

We all agreed on Mom's plan and went back to the stream. Unlike my usual trips to the stream, this time I had a frog sitting cross-legged on my head.

The trail ended at the stream, and I stopped to take my shoes and socks off and roll up my pants. My parents walked upstream.

"The merhorses live over there. Let's go!" Pip said as he wiggled nervously.

I plucked him off my head. "Hey!" he pouted.

"I can't see where you're pointing," I whispered. "Here, ride on my shoulder instead."

"The merhorses live over there," he repeated. This time, I could see him point toward the other side of the stream from where I had been looking for bugs this morning. Wait a minute. Wasn't that where I had seen that mysterious rainbow light earlier? Maybe I hadn't been imagining it after all!

I gave Sassafras a quick pet, and then carefully crossed the stream with Pip on my shoulder.

"We need to get over there to that log," Pip directed me. "You can sit on the shore there, and I'll dive down to get the merhorses."

"Get them from where?" I asked.

"From their rainbow cave, of course," replied Pip.

"Rainbow cave?" I breathed.

"Oh, right!" Pip clapped a webbed hand to his head. "You've never even seen a merhorse. Yes, they live deep down in the stream in hidden caves they built with rainbow stones."

"Wait a minute, are you telling me there are rainbow stones in our stream?" My heart beat a little faster at the thought.

"Well, yes and no," Pip said. "They aren't just lying around, if that's what you're thinking. When a merhorse finds a stone that's the right size and shape, it carries it back to the cave in its mouth. Then the merhorse uses magic to enchant the stone to shimmer in all the colors of the rainbow."

"Their caves sound amazing," I said dreamily. "That must be why they're hidden. I bet if the caves were near the top of the water, animals like raccoons could find them easily with that rainbow light shining out."

"Indeed," said Pip. "You're pretty smart for a human. You remind me a lot of your mother when she was your age. Ah, here we are. This log right here is the one we're looking for."

I knelt on the sandy shore. Pip hopped off my shoulder and jumped in with a *sploosh*. I got down on my hands and put my face right by the water. He disappeared under the log, but if I held my head in the right place, I could make out some rays of rainbow light shimmering deep below. I wished I had brought my underwater viewer. Next time, I promised myself.

Pip swam back into view. And something was following right behind him.

CHAPTER 7
PLEASE HELP!

The thing behind Pip was small, and the front half looked exactly like a miniature horse with light gray fur. Its white mane waved gently as two tiny hooves paddled through the water. Right around where its belly button would've been, it turned from a horse into a fish. The bottom part of its body was covered in dark green scales, and its powerful fishlike tail moved up and down as it swam. Its colors blended in with most things in the stream, so I doubted I would've spotted one on my own.

I put both hands in the water and watched in awe as it swam gracefully toward me. Pip climbed out of the water and sat on my wrist, while the merhorse glided into the palms of my hands. I started to lift it out of the water to take a closer look.

"Whoa! What are you doing?" Pip yelped in

alarm. "The merhorse needs to be underwater to breathe!"

"Oh!" I immediately lowered my hands. Now that they were back in the water, I could see flaps hidden by the horse fur on the merhorse's neck. They opened and closed over and over again. The merhorse had gills. Of course!

I leaned closer to it and said, "I'm so sorry! I didn't realize you had gills. I'll keep you in the water."

The merhorse moved its mouth as though it were

talking, but all I heard were some very strange, quiet sounds. I looked to Pip for help.

"Ah, yes. You don't speak merhorse. I'll translate."

Pip ran his hands down his purple skin and brushed off the rest of the water. He cleared his throat and began: "He said, 'Dear human girl, thank you for coming to help me and my fellow merhorses. We fear something is very wrong with our stream.'"

The merhorse continued talking. I turned to Pip.

Pip translated, "'Many days ago, we all felt our fur and scales burning and itching. Our eyes stung. It was hard to breathe. This horrible feeling continued the next day, and a few days later we had trouble finding mayflies to eat. After a while, the stinging in our eyes seemed to get better, but this morning it began once more.'"

Hmmm. I couldn't be positive yet, but from what the merhorse was saying, it seemed like the pollution was worse on the weekends. That could be a clue!

"I'm sorry to hear that," I said, leaning down toward the merhorse. "I also can't find any mayfly nymphs in the stream. My parents and I ran some tests on the stream water, and we think someone might be dumping soap into the stream."

The merhorse spoke again. Pip held a

hand to his mouth and gasped.

My stomach tightened. "What is it, Pip?"

Pip looked up at me with sad eyes. "He said, 'Can you find who it is? Can you get them to stop, please? I fear if things do not improve, we may starve. I do not know how many more days we can last here.'"

My heart dropped. We couldn't lose the merhorses too! "We'll find a way to fix the stream water. We have to. I'll be back soon to let you know what we figure out."

We *had* to save the merhorses. And quickly!

CHAPTER 8
SASSAFRAS?

I waded back to the opposite side of the stream with Pip once again on my shoulder.

He hopped down when we got to shore. "I'm really worried about those poor merhorses, Zoey. They're so hungry! I don't think I can find any mooflies, but someone in the forest might have something they can eat. I'll check back with you later?"

I gave a big sigh of relief. "That is a wonderful idea, Pip. They definitely need to eat. You work on that, and I'll try to figure out where the pollution is coming from."

Pip hopped into the forest. I opened my journal and added everything I'd just learned.

QUESTION:
Where is the stream pollutia coming from?

OBSERVATIONS:
Seems like soap is being dumped on weekends?

pollution started about a week ago.

I looked up to see my mom and dad coming toward me, but I didn't see Sassafras anywhere. He was probably hiding up in a tree again, freaked out that a drop of stream water might get on him.

"Sassafras?" I called. "Sassafras!"

Where *was* that cat?

My mom and dad joined me. "Sassafras," we all hollered.

Finally we heard a faraway "Meeoooooow!"

"What is Sassafras doing way down there?" I asked. We headed toward the distant meowing.

Every few feet we stopped and called "Sassafras!" And each time the meow got louder. We rounded a bend in the stream and found him balancing on a log. His tail was all fluffed up and he was growling at some white foam caught behind a log.

Wait . . . *foam!* Soap!

"Sassafras!" I said. "You found the soap!"

I ran over to pet him, and I noticed a pipe above his head.

"Mom! Dad! What is this weird pipe? It must be where the soap is coming from."

Mom bent down, swiped some of the soap foam, and sniffed it.

"Um, Mom? Why are you smelling it?"

Mom laughed. "That must look strange! I was checking to make sure that it wasn't natural foam. Sometimes when leaves and other bits of the forest break

down, they can make bubbles that look similar to soap bubbles. But there's no mistaking the smell of store-bought soap. Here, see what I mean?"

Mom put her foam-covered hand out to me, and I sniffed. It smelled sort of like dish soap. Definitely not at all like a forest or leaves or stream water.

"I still don't get it," I said peering into the pipe. "What is this pipe? Where is this water coming from?"

"It's stormwater," Mom and Dad said at the same time.

I looked at them, completely confused. Stormwater? It wasn't raining. And I was pretty sure that water from storms came from the sky and the clouds, and *not* from pipes in the ground.

"When it rains, what happens to the rain here in the forest?" Mom asked.

"It goes into the ground and makes mud and stuff?" I answered.

"Exactly," said Mom. "Now, what

happens when it rains on sidewalks and roads?"

"Hmmm." I thought. "It makes puddles? And it makes little rivers in the gutters?"

"Right, and where do those little rivers in the gutters go?" asked Mom.

I thought and thought, but I wasn't sure. I mean, the water must go somewhere. I needed my Thinking Goggles! I squinched my eyes tight,

pretended my Thinking Goggles were on my head, and tried to think about little rivers of water in gutters. I stretched and reached for a distant memory in my mind. There it was! My friend Sophie and I had been waiting by the side of the road for our bus in the pouring rain. We'd broken some sticks into little pieces and dropped them into the gutter river. The sticks zoomed along, and they went down into some sort of drain!

"Into a drain thingy!" I announced proudly.

"Yes, a storm drain," Mom said. "If we didn't have them, our roads and sidewalks would flood. Rain can't soak into sidewalks and roads like it can into the forest dirt. So we collect all the extra water in gutters and it goes into a storm drain —"

"And then it comes out here? At the stream?" I interrupted.

"Yes. So anything that's up there on the street can get gathered up by the rainwater and taken to a nearby stream or ocean. That's why we have to be careful about what we do on our streets and sidewalks."

I put my hands on my hips and looked up. "There's just one problem. It's not raining. So why is water coming out of this pipe? Is the water coming from a town far away where it's raining or something?"

"Great observation." My mom smiled. "No, it's definitely coming from somewhere nearby. Let's see if you can put this last piece of the puzzle together. What uses soap and water? A lot of it. Enough to fill a gutter with soapy water."

I wrinkled my nose in thought. I imagined a gutter river of soapy water. Hmmm. To make that much soapy water you'd have to wash something big. Really big. Like a boat or a . . . car!

"A car wash!" I shouted. Sassafras flew backward off the log. Whoops. I didn't mean to be quite that loud. But I was so excited. It had to be a car wash!

Mom and Dad nodded together, and I couldn't stop smiling. We could definitely fix this. First, we needed to find the car wash. That couldn't be too hard . . . Right?

CHAPTER 9
INTO TOWN

When we got home, we dropped off our things and our cat. Before we left on our hunt for a car wash, I quickly added some notes to my science journal.

OBSERVATION:
Soap is coming from the storm drain.

HYPOTHESIS:
The pollution is coming from a car wash!

Dad buckled in and started the car. He turned to Mom. "Where do you think I should drive first?"

I piped up from the backseat. "Shouldn't we start at Sam's Car Wash in town?" I mean, that seemed like a pretty obvious answer to me.

"Ah," my mom replied. "What would happen if the town car wash dumped soap into the storm drains all day long?"

Oh, I thought. "We would've had this problem from the beginning," I said. "There wouldn't be any merhorses in our stream!"

"Did you say . . . merhorses?" my dad asked.

"I meant to say *mayflies*," I said quickly. "There wouldn't be any mayflies."

"Correct," said Mom. "Which is why car washes like the one in town have special drains. All their soapy water travels through special pipes to a water treatment plant. There they remove the soap and grease from the water to keep our streams safer."

"So what are we looking for then? A person washing a car at their house?" I sighed. "That will be impossible to find!"

"No, something bigger than that. Although you're right, if you wash a car with a lot of soap at home, that soapy water goes down the road into a storm drain and into their local stream or ocean. But with all the damage to that part of the stream, I'm guessing we're looking for a group of kids running a car wash."

At first I was kind of mad at the kids. They were killing the mayfly babies and hurting the merhorses! Who would do that?

But then I realized *I* hadn't known that a car wash in town could hurt our stream, either. It's not like you can even see the stream from anywhere in town. Whoever these kids were, they probably had no idea what they were doing to our stream.

My dad drove up and down the streets in town. We looked everywhere. Just when we were about to give up, I saw a flash of neon. A sign that said . . . CAR WASH!

CHAPTER 10
YOU'VE GOT TO STOP!

The kids running the car wash were cleaning up for the day. We'd caught them just in time. We got out of the car and walked over. As we got closer, I realized they were *big* kids. Maybe even high schoolers.

One of the kids turned to us, and my mom sort of pushed me forward. Ummm, she expected me to talk to them? But they were so . . . tall.

The tall girl smiled down at me. "Oh,

hi. We're all done for the day, sorry. But we'll be here again next Saturday."

I swallowed. I glanced back at my parents, who nodded at me to go ahead. I took another step forward and cleared my throat.

"Uh, you can't do your car wash anymore," I squeaked out.

Now all the kids turned and stared at me. One boy laughed. He looked at my parents, but they didn't say anything. So he

bent down to me and asked, "Oh? Why not?"

"It's hurting the stream. It's killing the stream bugs, and it's really bad for the, um, *creatures* that live in the stream."

A few of the kids looked around. The girl who'd first talked pointed up and down the street. "But there's no stream here. See? It's just a parking lot. If

anything, it's making the ground nice and clean."

I turned to my parents again, but they only smiled at me. They really weren't going to help me out here, huh? Well, OK then.

"I know it sounds weird," I continued, "but here, come with me." I gestured and

the kids, now curious, followed me. "If we follow the soapy water from your car wash, you'll see what I mean."

I led them to the sidewalk and pointed down in the gutter, where a stream of soapy water was still traveling. We all walked along the sidewalk until I spotted the storm drain. The soapy water disappeared into the pipe right before our eyes.

"See? The soapy water travels in pipes underground, and then it pours into our stream. The soap foam from your car wash is polluting the water. The things that live in the stream aren't used to the soap chemicals. It's *killing* them."

"Whoa," said the boy. He looked up at my parents, who'd followed us to the storm drain. "Does this really go to the stream?"

"Yes, everything she said is true," said my mom. "We do need you to stop the car wash."

"Aw, man," said the boy. "We were

doing such a good job raising money for our class trip, though."

"We're almost halfway to our goal." The girl sighed. "But we don't want to pollute the stream. We had no idea."

"Honest, we didn't," added the boy.

I looked up at my mom and dad. "Isn't there something they could still do? Like maybe they could move their car wash to the parking lot at Sam's Car Wash. It has the special drains that don't take the soapy water to the stream, right?"

Mom thought for a minute. "Well, I

don't think they could use the parking lot at Sam's Car Wash. Although I seem to remember hearing that Sam's offers a fundraising program. Something about selling coupons." She turned to my dad. "Does that sound familiar?"

"I think I saw an article about that in the paper," he said. "Do you want me to call Sam's and check?"

The kids and I all said, "Yes!" at the same time. This would be great. A solution that helped the stream *and* the kids!

My dad called and talked to someone at Sam's. There were a lot of "mmm-hmms," and finally he flashed us a thumbs-up.

After the call, Dad gave the kids all the information, and my family headed home for dinner. I was starving after all that mystery-solving!

On our way home, though, I began to worry. We had stopped this car wash, but what about others? How could we keep other people from making the same mistake? Would the mayfly babies ever come back? And were we too late for the poor merhorses?

CHAPTER 11
PAINTING THE STREETS

"Ready?" I asked Dad. I balanced the can of white spray paint in my slippery gloved hands.

"Yep, you're all set." He pressed down the edges of the stencil one more time. "You shook it really well, right?"

"Yes, of *course* I did!" I stuck out my tongue.

He laughed and stepped way back next to my mom. I pressed down the top of the spray paint can, and white mist flew out. I kept spraying until you couldn't read the stencil anymore.

Next up was my favorite part. The big reveal! I set the can down and carefully peeled back the stencil.

My parents clapped. "Beautiful work!"

Right in front of the storm drain in bright white letters, there was now a message: DUMP NO WASTE. DRAINS TO STREAM.

I'd been so worried about the stream getting polluted with car wash soap again that my parents and I came up with a plan. Our city even had stencils and paint all ready for us. They just needed volunteers to drive around and paint the message on the storm drains.

Over the last several weeks, we'd spent an hour or two each Saturday and Sunday labeling storm drains in town. This was the last one!

As we drove home, I felt a great sense of relief. Now instead of the water from the gutter mysteriously disappearing, people could read about where it goes. They'd understand that whatever they put down there would end up in our stream.

We pulled into our driveway, and Mom let out a giant laugh. She quickly clapped her hand over her mouth.

"Are you OK?" my dad asked.

"Uh, yes. I, uh, thought I saw something on our doorstep." Mom reached back and squeezed my knee.

Something on our doorstep? Oh! *Something!* I squished my face against the window searching for Pip.

There he was, right on our doorstep. On Sassafras' head. I could tell that Sassafras was not pleased. His ears were out to the side, and he had a sour look on his face. I looked away so I wouldn't start cracking up.

Once my dad parked, I bolted out of the car. I pretended to bend down to tie my shoe. Pip hopped up onto my head. Sassafras let out a big breath of relief and bumped against me, purring in thanks.

"I thought you'd never get home!" Pip exclaimed. "The merhorses are requesting you down at the stream, Zoey."

"Are they OK?" I whispered up to Pip.

"Yes. They have news for you!" Pip said excitedly and gave a little jump on my head.

I sighed with relief. Pip had been able to find some grubs from the forest monsters to keep the merhorses comfortable. But apparently the merhorses weren't fond of forest grubs. We'd been trying to wait patiently for the mayfly nymphs to return.

Pip looked excited, so it had to be good news. I was hoping it was the best news! Which meant this would be the perfect time to finally snap a photo of my new friends.

I'd been down to visit the merhorses a few times, and I'd somehow managed to forget my camera every time. I desperately wanted a photo of the merhorses to add to my science journal.

I spun around to my parents and asked, "Can Sassafras and I go down to the stream?" Oops! I could feel Pip hanging on for dear life.

"Mmm-hmm," my mom managed to get out. She was pressing her lips together tightly to hold the laughs in.

I grabbed my underwater viewer and my camera from inside and – careful not to make any more sudden turns – Sassafras, Pip, and I set out for the stream.

CHAPTER 12
A GIFT!

Once we were in the forest, I couldn't hold back my questions anymore. "Why did the merhorses send for me? What's the news? Are the mayfly nymphs back?"

"You'll see for yourself in a moment," Pip called down from my head as he gave it a little pat.

I slowly waded across the stream while Sassafras grumbled and sat on the shore to wait. We made it to the log, and Pip leapt into the water.

I set my things down, pressed my underwater viewer into the water, and gasped. I would never get used to the beauty of the shimmering rainbow glow from deep under the log. I could only see the entrance to the cave from up here (I wasn't quite brave enough to stick my whole head under the cold stream water yet), but it was breathtaking. Each small stone sent out rays of light. The colors smoothly changed from red to orange to yellow . . . all the way through the rainbow and back to red again. I couldn't take my eyes off the magical light show.

At least not until Pip cleared his throat. "Zoey, I know the rainbow cave is really something, but I've got someone here who'd like to talk to you."

Of course! The merhorses! I quickly put away my underwater viewer and turned my attention to the water. There, waiting patiently, was the merhorse. I set my hands in the water, and he swam into my palms. I smiled. Since the first time I'd met him, his eyes had grown so much brighter, and his whole body seemed to have a new sparkle to it. It was such a relief to see how much the merhorses had improved since we'd fixed the stormwater problem.

The merhorse spoke. I turned to Pip.

"He says, 'I have wonderful news to share with you, Zoey. The mayfly nymphs have begun to reappear. Our stomachs are full, and we are happy once again. We are so grateful to you for saving us. We want to present you with a gift to show our thanks.'"

I nodded eagerly and opened my

hands underwater so he could swim away. I was so excited. I love presents. And I couldn't think of anything more amazing than a present from a merhorse!

I didn't realize that I was holding my breath until I saw a whole wave of shimmering motion in the stream.

"Woooooowwww." Pip and I both exhaled.

At least a dozen beautiful, healthy merhorses swim-galloped toward me, their long manes waving in the water. All of them seemed to have bigger cheeks than usual, like chipmunks with mouths full of seeds. They lined up and paddled in place, looking up at me with big, bright eyes.

I held out my hands in the water.

One by one, each merhorse

carefully placed a magically sparkling rainbow stone in my hands.

Pip leaned so far forward, he fell in the water by accident. His cheeks were red as he hopped back onto shore and brushed off the stream water.

For a moment, all I could do was stare open-mouthed at the amazing scene before me. Merhorses. Rainbow stones.

It was all too much! But then I remembered my manners. I looked each merhorse in the eyes and said, "Thank you so much for the beautiful gift."

I leaned back a little to take a closer look at the stones and bumped into my camera. Oh! My camera! "Would you mind if I took a quick photo of you to add to my science journal?" I asked nervously.

The merhorses looked at each other, nodded, and then faced me. I could see bubbles coming out of their mouths, but I had no idea what they were saying.

Pip pointed toward the water. "Aren't you going to take the photo? They're saying, 'Cheese!'"

"Oh!" I carefully placed the rainbow stones in my pocket, scrambled for my camera, and snapped a picture. I smiled

down at the photo of my sweet little magical friends. "Thank you, merhorses!"

The first merhorse I'd met came close again and said something. Pip translated, "'We must head back to our young in the rainbow cave now. But we thank you for saving us. We hope you will visit us again.'"

Pip and I sat on the shore and watched the herd of merhorses gracefully swim-gallop into the darkness under the log. I pulled the magic stones out of my pocket and stared some more.

Pip reached out a webbed hand and rolled one of the rainbow stones around in my hand. "I have never heard of the merhorses giving these away. You're very lucky."

I thought for a moment, and then took one of the stones and held it out to Pip. "You were a big help, Pip. I want you to have one."

Pip's eyes teared up a bit, and he grabbed my wrist in a big hug. "Thank you, Zoey! I'm going to take this straight home

so I don't lose it." He popped the stone into one of his cheeks and gave me a big smile.

I kissed the top of his head, and then waved as Pip hopped back to his home in the forest.

Sassafras was waiting for me on the other side of the stream. Before I put my socks and shoes on, I carefully set the rainbow stones next to me on the sandy shore. Sassafras stared at them, and his eyes got really big. He started to purr. It was so beautiful and calming to watch the rainbow lights.

"Oh man, Mom has probably never seen rainbow stones. We've gotta go show her, Sassafras!" I grabbed all my stuff, and we set off for the house at a run.

CHAPTER 13

A RAINBOW ROOM

I burst through the door and hollered, "Mom! Where are you? You've got to come see these!"

I smiled up at Mom and held out two closed fists.

"What is it, Zoey? Was everything OK down at the stream?" Mom asked.

Instead of answering, I turned my fists over and opened my hands to reveal the rainbow stones. The room filled with rays of shimmering rainbow light.

"Ohhhhhhh." Mom reached a finger out to touch them. "What are those?"

"A gift from the merhorses," I whispered. "Enchanted rainbow stones. Their caves are decorated with these. Aren't they the most beautiful things you've ever seen?"

Mom carefully rolled one into her hand and stared.

We were so mesmerized by the stones that we jumped when Dad walked over to us.

"What are you two up to?" Dad asked. He glanced at the stones in our hands and gave us a strange look. "Um, why are we staring at these little rocks like they're precious gems?"

Poor Dad! He couldn't see the rainbow at all. He was really missing out.

"Oh, I got them down at the stream. I think they're really special," I said. "I'll go put them in my room."

"Sure. Dinner's almost ready." Dad picked up one of the stones and turned it first one way and then the other. "Huh," he said and placed it back in my hand.

I went to my room and set the rainbow stones in a line on my desk. I turned off the light and stared in awe at the rainbow that shone on my walls. "This is so cool," I whispered.

Sassafras jumped up on my desk and started rolling one of the rainbow stones around between his paws.

"No, kitty! I don't want to lose them!" I plucked him off the desk.

His legs spun around like a windmill as he tried to get back to the stones. One of his legs bopped my science journal and flipped it open. I grinned as the rainbow light shone down on a blank page, ready for our next adventure.

GLOSSARY

Algae: A green, slimy plant that grows in water. You can find a lot of algae in water that gets a lot of sun or that has pollution.

Caddisfly: An insect that lives in water when it's a nymph and builds a shelter on its back out of mud and rocks, sticks, or leaves.

Hypothesis: What you think is going to happen.

Mayfly: An insect that lives in water when it's a nymph and is very sensitive to pollution.

Nymph: A kind of baby insect.

pH: A way that you can check for pollution. If the pH in water is too high or too low, that means something has been added to the water.

Storm drain: Where the water and stuff from streets and sidewalks goes. It ends up in streams, lakes, or oceans.

ABOUT THE AUTHOR AND ILLUSTRATOR

ASIA CITRO used to be a science teacher, but now she plays at home with her two kids and writes books. When she was little, she had a cat just like Sassafras. He loved to eat bugs and always made her laugh (his favorite toy was a plastic human nose that he carried everywhere). Asia has also written three activity books: *150+ Screen-Free Activities for Kids, The Curious Kid's Science Book,* and *A Little Bit of Dirt.* She has yet to find a baby dragon in her backyard, but she always keeps an eye out, just in case.

MARION LINDSAY is a children's book illustrator who loves stories and knows a good one when she reads it. She likes to draw anything and everything but does spend a completely unfair amount of time drawing cats. Sometimes she has to draw dogs just to make up for it. She illustrates picture books and chapter books as well as painting paintings and designing patterns. Like Asia, Marion is always on the lookout for dragons and sometimes thinks there might be a small one living in the airing cupboard.

for activities and more visit
ZOEYANDSASSAFRAS.COM